Gabriella's playtime

Brian Knapp

Illustrations by David Woodroffe

A (Curriculum Visions) Citizenship book from Atlantic Europe Publishing

Teacher's Resources
There is a teacher's resource to accompany this book, available only from the publisher.
Resources include photocopiable worksheets, lesson plans and curriculum correlation.

Cherry Court Kids CD-Rom
A CD-Rom featuring all six of the Cherry Court Kids is available only from the publisher.

Dedicated Web Site
There's more about other great Curriculum Visions packs and a wealth of supporting
information available at our dedicated web site:
www.CurriculumVisions.com

Atlantic Europe Publishing

First published in 2003 by Atlantic
Europe Publishing Company Ltd

Copyright © 2003
Atlantic Europe Publishing Company Ltd

Author
Brian Knapp, BSc, PhD

Art Director
Duncan McCrae, BSc

Illustrator
David Woodroffe

Editor
Gillian Gatehouse

Senior Designer
Adele Humphries, BA

Acknowledgements
The publishers would like to thank
Kezia Humphries and *Pauline Whitehouse*
for their help and advice.

Designed and produced by
Earthscape Editions

Printed in Hong Kong by
Wing King Tong

**Gabriella's playtime
– Curriculum Visions**
A CIP record for this book is
available from the British Library

Paperback ISBN 186214 335 8
Hardback ISBN 186214 337 4

Contents

It's playtime!......................................4

It's my game..6

Forbidden stairs........................8

Lost treasure..........................10

An accident occurs 12

Out of bounds 14

The baby bird 16

Playing dare 18

Ouch! 20

Lining up 22

What Gabriella has learned....24

Gabriella knows that tidy up time means it is nearly playtime.

 4

It's playtime!

It's the middle of the morning and Gabriella is looking forward to playtime.

At long last teacher says, "It's tidy up time".

Gabriella wants to go out to play as quickly as she can. What should Gabriella do?

Choose what Gabriella should do:

① Run out of the class as soon as she has tidied up.

② Wait for the teacher to tell her what to do.

③ Ask her teacher if she can leave once she has tidied up.

or...

④ Can you think of something else?

5

Gabriella wants to choose the game.

It's my game

Gabriella goes across to a group of her friends.

Maria is one of the group and has chosen the game.

Gabriella wants to play a different game. What should Gabriella do?

Choose what Gabriella should do:

① Tell her friends they should play Gabriella's game.

② Go and find some other friends to play with.

③ Join in Maria's game.

or...

④ Can you think of something else?

Some older boys are breaking the rules.

 8

Forbidden stairs

Gabriella looks across the playground and sees some older boys playing on the stairs.

No one is allowed to play on the stairs, but the teacher hasn't noticed. What should Gabriella do?

Gabriella finds a necklace in the playground.

Lost treasure

In the middle of a game, Gabriella sees something sparkling on the playground floor.

She finds it is a necklace and shows it to her friends.

The necklace does not belong to any of her friends. What should Gabriella do?

Choose what Gabriella should do:

① Keep the necklace for herself.

② Leave the necklace on the floor.

③ Hang the necklace on the fence.

or...

④ Can you think of something else?

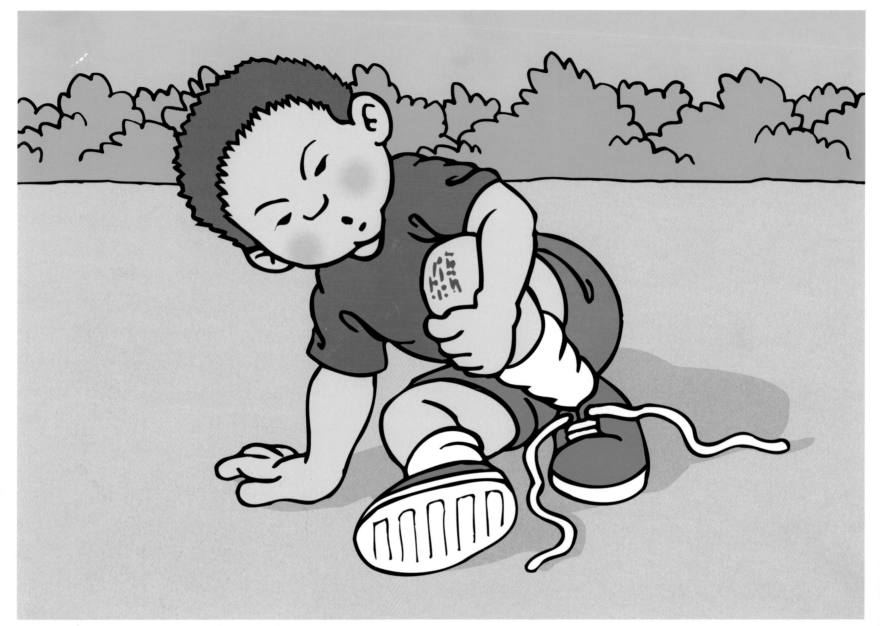

Frank grazes his knee.

An accident occurs

Frank is playing football but he doesn't notice that his shoelace is coming undone.

He trips on his shoelace, falls over and grazes his knee.

Gabriella is nearby. What should she do?

Choose what Gabriella should do:

① Tell Frank to go to the first aid room.

② Tell Frank to grow up and forget it.

③ Take Frank to the playground teacher.

or...

④ Can you think of something else?

13

The ball goes over the fence.

Out of bounds

Fariq and Dave are kicking a ball to one another on the playing field.

Fariq kicks too hard and the ball sails over the fence and outside the school grounds.

Fariq says to Gabriella, "Can you go and fetch that ball?". What should Gabriella do?

Choose what Gabriella should do:

① Tell Fariq to go outside the school and pick up the ball.

② Tell the teacher the ball is lost.

③ Tell Fariq she is not allowed to go out of the playground.

or...

④ Can you think of something else?

Gabriella finds a baby bird that has fallen from its nest.

The baby bird

Gabriella and some friends are collecting leaves by the hedge.

Suddenly they spot a baby bird that has fallen out of a nest in the hedge.

They can see its big eyes looking at them for help.

What should Gabriella do?

Choose what Gabriella should do:

① Walk away.

② Tell the playground teacher.

③ Put it back in its nest.

or...

④ Can you think of something else?

17

Lizzie asks Gabriella to be naughty, too.

Playing dare

Lizzie likes to be naughty. During playtime she runs in and out of the school. This is against the rules.

Lizzie dares Gabriella to run in and out of the school, too.

What should Gabriella do?

Choose what Gabriella should do:

1. Accept the dare.

2. Tell Lizzie it is against the rules.

3. Tell Lizzie that she won't be her friend any more if she keeps being naughty.

or...

4. Can you think of something else?

Darren is pulling Gabriella's hair.

Ouch!

Gabriella is talking to her friends when Darren comes up behind her.

Without any warning he reaches over and tugs at her hair.

It hurts and Gabriella cries out.

What should Gabriella do?

Choose what Gabriella should do:

① Slap Darren.

② Move away.

③ Tell Darren to stop it.

or...

④ Can you think of something else?

21

Gill and Dave spoil the line for everyone else.

Lining up

It is the end of playtime and the whistle has gone. Everyone lines up in rows. The ones who line up best get to go in first.

Gabriella wants her class to go in first, but Gill and Dave keep talking. Because of this, Gabriella's class goes in last. What should Gabriella do?

Choose what Gabriella should do:

① Tell them off by going "shhhhhhhh!".

② Get their friends not to talk to them until they behave.

③ Wait for the teacher to do something.

or…

④ Can you think of something else?

Gabriella has learned these things:

- To play with others.

- Not to boss others about.

- To stay within the rules.

- To hand in lost property.

- To care about all living things.

- Not to allow herself to be bullied.

- To get other people to help when things go wrong.

Do you know that it is important always to stay safely inside the school grounds?

Do you try to get on with your friends?

Do you help others with their problems?